FOREWORD

by Charley Parker

What do high-tech minisubs, a 200-year-old parrot that speaks 70 languages, Christopher Columbus, extinct plesiosaurs and mysterious warriors from a lost undersea civilization have in common?

The answer is Capt'n Eli.

Capt'n Eli, quite simply, is a treat. Artist/writer Jay Piscopo has created a story with its roots in the adventure comics of a simpler age, but flowering in the digital space of the Internet. It's an unexpected treasure.

Ever since I started my web comic, *Argon Zark!,* back in the Internet stone age of 1995, I've watched the community of independent comics grow.

Whether in print or online, independently produced comics have presented creators with a truly daunting challenge, essentially: "You're on your own, kids, let's see what you can do." There are no boundaries and no rules. Independent creators have the freedom to call their own shots and create the best comics they know how to do. This is a great opportunity and also a real test of creators' skills and dedication.

This is why a comic like Capt'n Eli is such a treat. Jay's pages are brimming with the kind of unpretentious fun and enthusiasm that makes me remember why I liked comics so much when I was a kid.

A delightfully improbable mix of Silver Age adventure comics, Jonny Quest, Aquaman, The Sub-Mariner, *seaQuest, Star Wars, 20,000 Leagues Under the Sea* and maybe even a little bit of *Argon Zark!*, Jay's undersea sci-fi/fantasy/adventure/mystery stories do what good comics do best: entertain.

The focus is on fun. As soon as we dive into a Capt'n Eli story we're immersed in a sea of underwater mysteries, high-tech ships, flying mini-subs, time travel, lost civilizations, undersea empires, monsters, robots, mysterious foes and equally mysterious allies. In short, a tasty recipe for adventure-comics stew.

The stories unfold through an imaginative blend of solid comics drawing and artfully crafted 3-D modeling and special effects. The popularity of anime has made many of us more comfortable with this kind of stylistic combination, and I'm personally quite fond of it (as anyone who's seen my work knows). I think it's really enjoyable when done well, and Jay Piscopo is one of the few comics artists who does it well.

He also brings that level of attention to the creation of the settings and vessels in the stories. (I love the Hydrons' sinister Nautilus-like subs.) He uses the renderings to advantage to place the action in a realm of science fiction and fantasy landscapes, er... seascapes. But, unlike many comics artists who become fascinated and distracted with their 3-D graphics, Jay knows that the art is always in support of telling a good story. His emphasis on timeless storytelling values works nicely both in print and on the web.

So for those of you who are diving with Capt'n Eli and crew for the first time in this print edition, welcome aboard! And, as Commander X instructs us heartily on the intro page of the Capt'n Eli web site, "Stand by for adventure!"

Charley Parker
Creator of *Argon Zark!*

www.argonzark.com

HEY, EVERYBODY!
MY NAME IS CAPT'N ELI, INVENTOR AND EXPLORER.
LIKE A LOT OF FOLKS, I'M FASCINATED BY MARITIME MYSTERIES.
GUESS I'M SO INTERESTED 'CAUSE I'M A MARITIME MYSTERY MYSELF.
HERE'S THE STORY OF HOW I GOT STARTED. THE ONGOING SAGA OF...
THE MYSTERY OF ME!

THE UNDERSEA ADVENTURES OF CAPT'N ELI

THE POD KEPT ME ALIVE IN A STATE OF SUSPENDED ANIMATION. A KIND OF ENDLESS SLEEP.

SO WHO KNOWS HOW LONG OR HOW FAR I TRAVELED?

MY EARLIEST MEMORY IS THE SOUND OF A LULLABY AND THE MUSIC OF WHALES SINGING.

THE TUNE WAS PLAYED BY THE POD'S COMPUTER. THE COMPUTER NOT ONLY KEPT ME ALIVE, BUT PROTECTED ME FROM ALL THE PERILS OF THE SEA WITH ITS ADVANCED TECHNOLOGY.

I'VE MADE GUESSES ABOUT WHERE I COME FROM: A TOP SECRET PROJECT, ATLANTIS, EVEN OUTER SPACE!

THE ONLY CLUES ARE THE POD AND A FUNNY LITTLE TUNE IN MY HEAD.

TO THIS DAY, I'M STILL SEARCHING FOR WHO PUT ME IN THE POD AND WHY.

THE MYSTERY OF ME

POPS TOOK ME TO HIS WIFE, WHO I CAME TO CALL MA. MA TOOK ONE LOOK AT ME AND GOT AN IDEA.

MA AND POPS CALLED ME THEIR SON AND NAMED ME ELI AFTER POPS'S DAD. AS I GREW, THEY REALIZED I WASN'T LIKE OTHER KIDS, I NEEDED TO BE ON OR IN THE OCEAN!

GLUB!

I COULD STAY UNDER LONGER THAN MOST GROWN-UPS!

AS I GREW OLDER, I LOVED TO TINKER. I'D GATHER MACHINE PARTS FROM POPS'S JUNKYARD AND INVENT STUFF.

I DON'T THINK POPS REALIZED WHAT HE GOT HIMSELF INTO WHEN HE TAUGHT ME HOW TO SAIL.

MA AND POPS SAID I NEEDED TO LEARN RESPONSIBILITY AND HOW TO STAY ON LAND FOR A WHILE.
WOOP!
SO THEY GAVE ME THE BEST PRESENT AND THE BEST FRIEND I HAVE.

I NAMED HIM BARNEY. WHY BARNEY? I DON'T KNOW, HE JUST LOOKS LIKE A BARNEY. WELL, BARNEY AND I GOT ALONG LIKE BUTTER AND POPCORN.

I READ BOOKS ON DOG TRAINING AND BARNEY WAS THE PERFECT STUDENT.
OK, BARNEY, TIE A BOWLINE KNOT.

ARF!

GOOD BOY! LET'S GO GET THE SAILBOAT!

WELL, AFTER THAT, POPS MADE ME AND BARNEY PROMISE NOT TO TAKE THE SAILBOAT.
SO I STARTED A SPECIAL PROJECT.

RIGHT AFTER BREAKFAST I REVEALED MY PLAN TO BUILD MY OWN SUBMARINE.
THE "GUPPY"
MA SAID SOMETHING ABOUT "IRONIC," A WORD I STILL DON'T UNDERSTAND,
AND POPS SAID SOMETHING ABOUT "THE TRUTH."

THE TRUTH WAS THE POD.
AND THE TRUTH WAS MA AND POPS WEREN'T MY PARENTS.
POPS SAID HE AND MA THOUGHT WHOEVER PUT ME IN THE POD, BEING SO ADVANCED AND ALL...

WOULD FIND ME A LOT EASIER THAN IF HE WENT LOOKING FOR THEM.
THEY NEVER CAME LOOKING.

I LEARNED TWO THINGS THAT DAY:
JUST BECAUSE YOU DON'T HAVE SOMEONE'S BLOOD DOESN'T MEAN YOU AREN'T FAMILY, AND
I KNEW MY ORIGIN AND DESTINY WERE CONNECTED TO THE SEA.

AFTER A FEW WEEKS, IT WAS DONE.
POPS HELPED ON SOME OF THE WELDING AND I INCORPORATED THE POD'S COMPUTER AS WELL AS POPS'S NAVY SURPLUS HARDWARE.
I NAMED HER THE GUPPY.
THE GUPPY RAN ON SODIUM BATTERIES THAT GAINED POWER FROM THE SALT IN THE OCEAN ITSELF.
AND WITH HER HONEYCOMB STEEL FRAME, WE COULD GO ANYWHERE- NO MATTER HOW FAR OR DEEP.
OUR FIRST VOYAGE
WAS TO VOLCANO ISLAND.
THERE, WE MET JOLLY ROGER, A 200-YEAR-OLD PARROT
WHO SPEAKS 70 LANGUAGES!
GOT ANY GRAPES?
HOW WE MET IS A WHOLE OTHER STORY I'LL TELL SOMETIME.
ANYWAY, ROGER ASKED TO JOIN BARNEY AND ME,
AND WE BECAME A TEAM!

ONE NIGHT, A HURRICANE HIT.
A NAVY SUB IS DAMAGED SOMEWHERE NEAR EAGLE ROCK!
...ALL CONTACT HAS BEEN LOST, SEARCH CREWS ARE HAMPERED BY A RELENTLESS HURRICANE. OFFICIALS ARE CONCERNED TIME IS RUNNING OUT....
LOST SUB
POPS DIDN'T WANT ME TO GO. I CONVINCED HIM THAT THE GUPPY COULD FIND THE SUB,

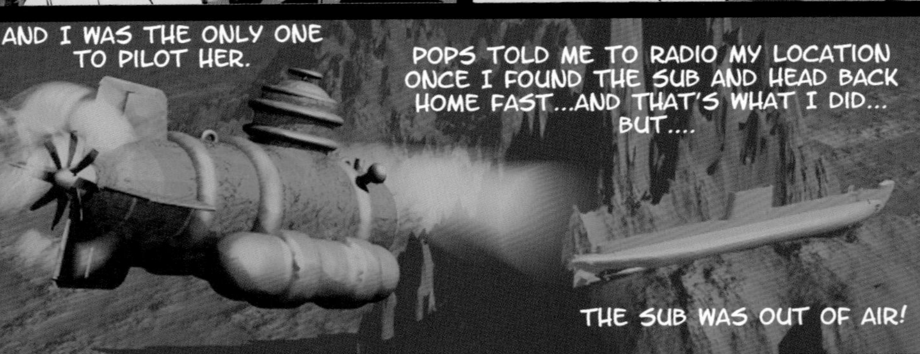
AND I WAS THE ONLY ONE TO PILOT HER.
POPS TOLD ME TO RADIO MY LOCATION ONCE I FOUND THE SUB AND HEAD BACK HOME FAST...AND THAT'S WHAT I DID... BUT....
THE SUB WAS OUT OF AIR!

I COULD HEAR THE SAILORS RAPPING MORSE CODE AGAINST THE HULL.
TIME RAN OUT!
I DEPLOYED AN OLD ANCHOR CHAIN AND HOPED THE GUPPY'S ENGINE COULD TAKE IT!

THE GUPPY WAS DOIN' FINE...
SNAP!
THE CHAIN WAS ANOTHER MATTER.

"A CHAIN IS ONLY AS STRONG AS ITS WEAKEST LINK."
BOY, DID I LEARN WHAT THAT MEANT!
MY OPTIONS HAD RUN OUT...
I'VE GOT TO GET THAT CHAIN OR THOSE SAILORS ARE DOOMED!

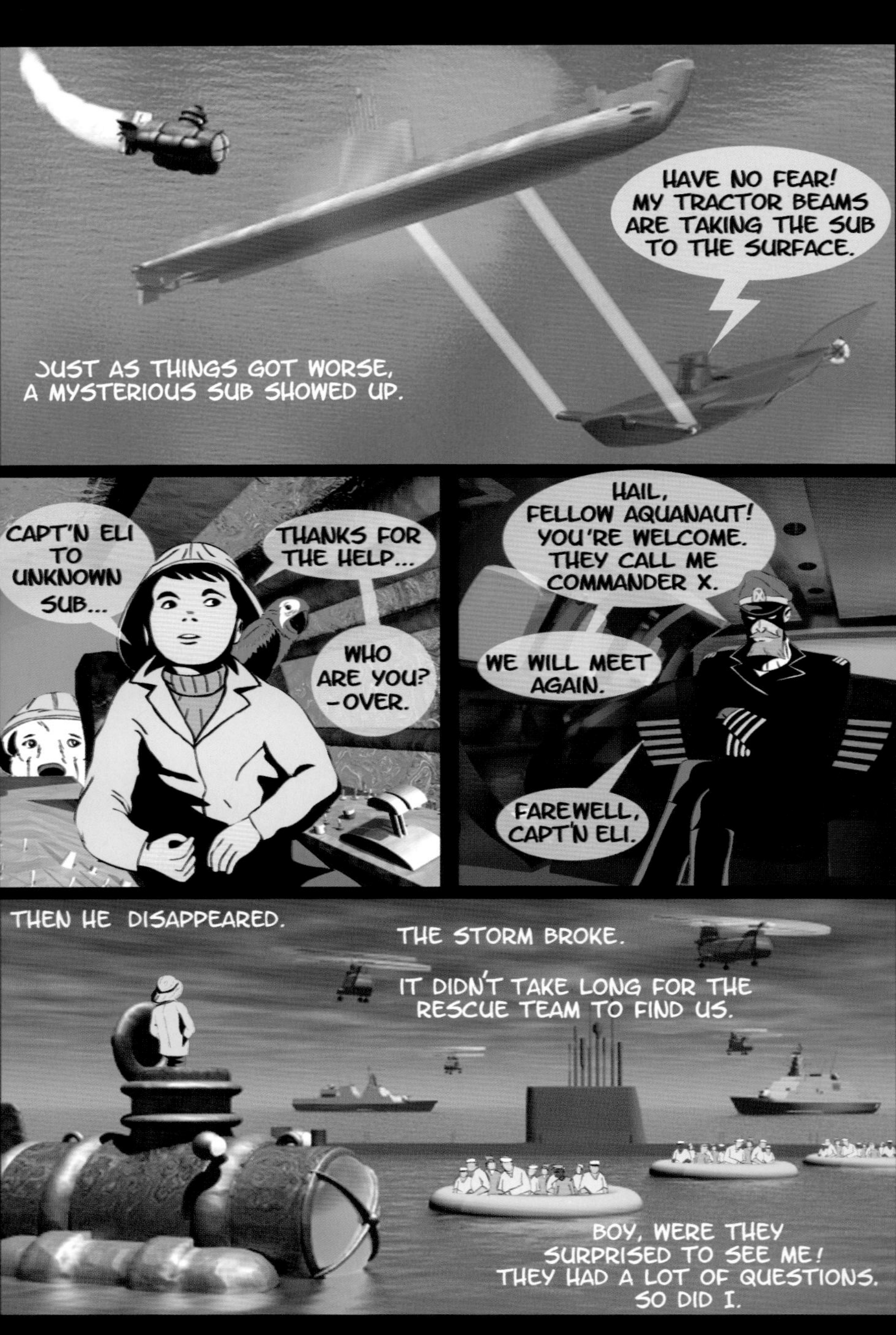
HAVE NO FEAR! MY TRACTOR BEAMS ARE TAKING THE SUB TO THE SURFACE.
JUST AS THINGS GOT WORSE, A MYSTERIOUS SUB SHOWED UP.
CAPT'N ELI TO UNKNOWN SUB...
THANKS FOR THE HELP...
WHO ARE YOU? -OVER.
HAIL, FELLOW AQUANAUT! YOU'RE WELCOME. THEY CALL ME COMMANDER X.
WE WILL MEET AGAIN.
FAREWELL, CAPT'N ELI.
THEN HE DISAPPEARED.
THE STORM BROKE.
IT DIDN'T TAKE LONG FOR THE RESCUE TEAM TO FIND US.
BOY, WERE THEY SURPRISED TO SEE ME! THEY HAD A LOT OF QUESTIONS. SO DID I.

THE FIRST THING I WANTED TO KNOW WAS, WHO IS COMMANDER X?
THE NAVY TOLD ME THAT THEY THOUGHT HE WAS A DESCENDENT OF CAPTAIN NEMO HIMSELF!
LIKE NEMO, CMDR. X EXPLORES THE DEPTHS IN AN ADVANCED SUB WITH A DISTINCT HAMMERHEAD DESIGN CALLED "SUB X."
CMDR. X WAS A HERO IN WWII FIGHTING FOR THE ALLIES, BUT, LIKE CAPTAIN NEMO, HE BECAME DISSATISFIED WITH THE SURFACE WORLD AND, IN LATER YEARS, WAS THOUGHT OF AS A VILLAIN.
WHICH IS WHY I UNFORTUNATELY ENDED UP GETTING CREDIT FOR THE RESCUE.

I TOLD 'EM ABOUT CMDR. X, BUT THEY WOULDN'T LISTEN....
THE DAILY WORLD
MARINE MARVEL SAVES SUB!
THE GLOBE TODAY
SUB-BOY!
CAPT'N ELI HAS BEEN INVITED
TO THE NAVY'S ADVANCED SUB RESEARCH LAB TO SHARE INSIGHTS ON...
THINGS DIDN'T GO SO GREAT AT THE LAB....
I DON'T KNOW HOW I DID IT, COMMODORE, I JUST DID IT.
THIS IS IMPOSSIBLE! HIS SCHEMATIC IS IN CRAYON!
NOW, KLAUS...
I MISSED POPS AND MA, SO I LEFT THE BIG BRASS TO SORT THINGS OUT ON THEIR OWN.
WHEN I GOT BACK, THEY WERE SO GLAD TO SEE ME!
THEY HAD A LETTER FROM THE FAMOUS EXPLORATION TEAM, THE SEASEARCHERS, AND IT WAS ADDRESSED TO ME!
I COULDN'T BELIEVE IT, THE LETTER WAS AN INVITATION TO JOIN THE TEAM!

SHE SAID I SHOULD STAY AT HOME, THAT IT WAS TOO DANGEROUS FOR A CHILD, AND I'D HAVE PLENTY OF TIME FOR ADVENTURE WHEN I WAS GROWN.

AFTER MA HAD HER SAY, POPS STARED OUT AT THE OCEAN FOR A WHILE, THEN HE SAID...

"OUR LITTLE CAPT'N HERE BUILT HIMSELF A SUBMARINE AT AGE NINE. HE TAUGHT HIS DOG HOW TO TIE KNOTS -- AND THEY HOLD!

NOT TO MENTION HIS WELL-TRAVELED PARROT...

I THINK THE LITTLE FELLA CAN TAKE CARE OF HIMSELF."

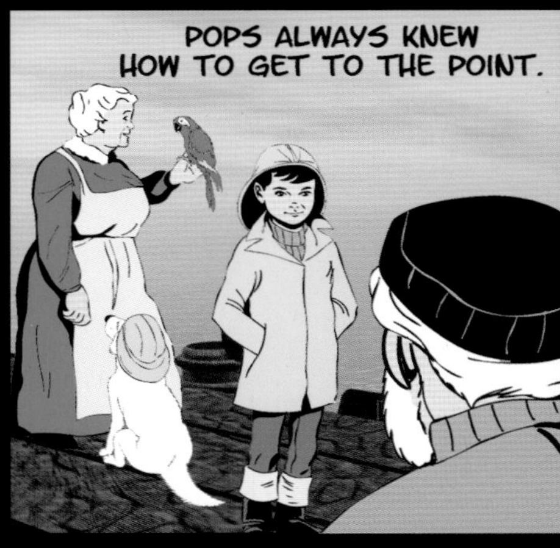

I HATE GOODBYES...
AND ALWAYS WEAR YOUR RAINCOAT...
MAKE SURE TO WRITE...
I WILL...

THERE ARE TWO THINGS I DON'T WANT YOU TO FORGET:
THE WORLD IS YOUR OYSTER, SON, AND WHEREVER YOU GO,
THIS WILL ALWAYS BE YOUR HOME.

SEE WHY I HATE GOODBYES? ALWAYS MUSHY! BUT I KNEW I WAS GOING TO MISS THEM.
BARNEY AND ROGER WERE SECURE IN THE GUPPY. I STARTED THE ENGINE.

AS EAGLE ROCK DISAPPEARED FROM VIEW, I COULD STILL SPOT MA AND POPS ON THE DOCK.

ON THE WAY TO THE MEETING WITH THE SEASEARCHERS I HAD SOME TIME TO KILL, SO WE WENT EXPLORING.

WE MET A MAN NAMED GAROO WHO PEOPLE CALLED "THE ISLANDER." THEY SAID HE HAD STRANGE POWERS AND COULD TELL THE FUTURE.
I ASKED HIM IF I WOULD LEARN ABOUT MY PAST.
HE SAID, "WHAT YOU SEEK WILL ALWAYS BE ONE STEP AHEAD AND ONE STEP BEHIND YOU." THEN HE WALKED INTO THE JUNGLE.

ROGER WASN'T IMPRESSED.
WHAT'S WITH THAT GAROO GUY?
I'VE READ BETTER FORTUNE COOKIES!
HE'S OK, ROGER.
WE ARRIVED AT THE COORDINATES AND WAITED. I GOT A FEELING THIS WAS GOING TO BE BIG!

BIG MIGHT NOT BE THE RIGHT WORD
TO DESCRIBE THE SEASEARCHER SUB...
HOW ABOUT ENORMOUS ?!

NEXT TO THE SEASEARCHERS'S SUB, THE GUPPY IS APPROPRIATELY NAMED!
AHOY, CAPT'N ELI, WELCOME ABOARD THE SEASCAPE!
PROFESSOR WOW IS A REALLY NEAT GUY. BARNEY AND ROGER LIKE HIM. AND I LIKE HIM, TOO.
PROF. WOW TOOK ME ON A TOUR OF THE SEASCAPE, WHICH HE DESIGNED,
AND TOLD ME ABOUT THE SEASEARCHERS'S MISSION TO EXPLORE THE UNKNOWN.
PROF. WOW SAID HE WISHED THE SEASEARCHERS COULD HAVE HELPED THE SUB RESCUE,
BUT THEY WERE AWAY ON ANOTHER MISSION. HE WAS IMPRESSED WITH THE GUPPY'S DESIGN AND ASKED IF I'D LIKE TO JOIN THE SEASEARCHERS!
I SAID YES IN A HEARTBEAT.
I TOLD PROF. WOW ABOUT MY POD AND HE AGREED TO HELP ME FIND MY ORIGIN.
WE ARRIVED IN ANTARCTICA AT ONE OF THE SEASEARCHER BASES.
THERE I MET REST OF THE TEAM.

AND NOW THAT YOU'VE MET CAPT'N ELI LET ME INTRODUCE...

GLAD TO HAVE YOU ALONG!
DR. AMELIA BOLO, PILOT AND INVENTOR OF THE HYDROCOPTER.

RED PEPPER, ENGINEER
DESIGNER AND PILOT OF THE EARTHSUB.
NEED ANYTHING, CAPT'N? JUST ASK!

CMDR. MARK FATHOM, PILOT OF THE TRIDENT
AND OUR SECURITY CHIEF.
PLEASURE TO SERVE WITH YOU.

ELI HAS SIGNED ON AS OUR NEW MINI-SUB PILOT. HE HAS DESIGNED ONE OF THE MOST AMAZING SUBMERSIBLES I HAVE EVER SEEN! LET ME SHOW YOU....

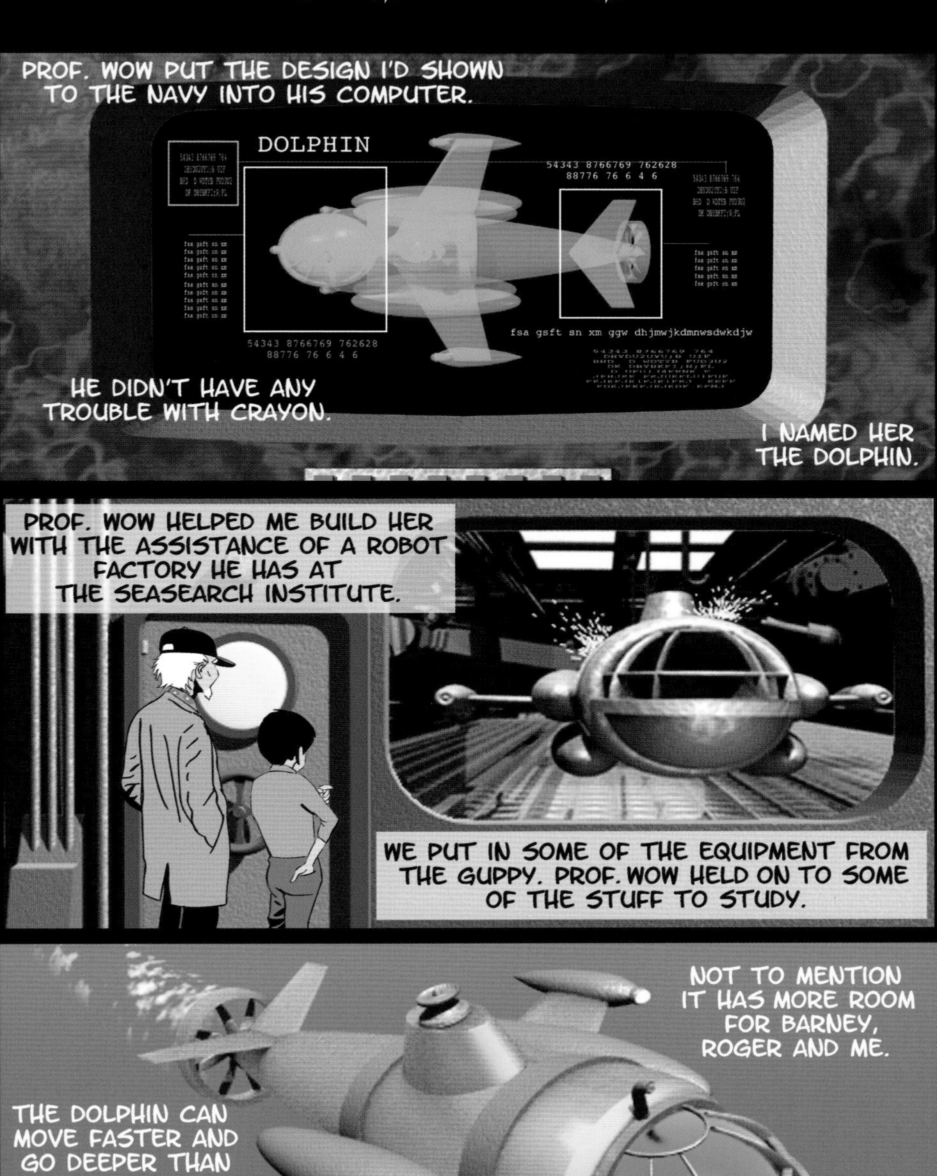
PROF. WOW PUT THE DESIGN I'D SHOWN TO THE NAVY INTO HIS COMPUTER.
DOLPHIN
54343 8766769 762628
88776 76 6 4 6
fsa gsft sn xm ggw dhjmwjkdmnwsdwkdjw
54343 8766769 762628
88776 76 6 4 6
HE DIDN'T HAVE ANY TROUBLE WITH CRAYON.
I NAMED HER THE DOLPHIN.
PROF. WOW HELPED ME BUILD HER WITH THE ASSISTANCE OF A ROBOT FACTORY HE HAS AT THE SEASEARCH INSTITUTE.
WE PUT IN SOME OF THE EQUIPMENT FROM THE GUPPY. PROF. WOW HELD ON TO SOME OF THE STUFF TO STUDY.
NOT TO MENTION IT HAS MORE ROOM FOR BARNEY, ROGER AND ME.
THE DOLPHIN CAN MOVE FASTER AND GO DEEPER THAN THE GUPPY.
IT CAN EVEN BECOME AIRBORNE FOR A LIMITED TIME!

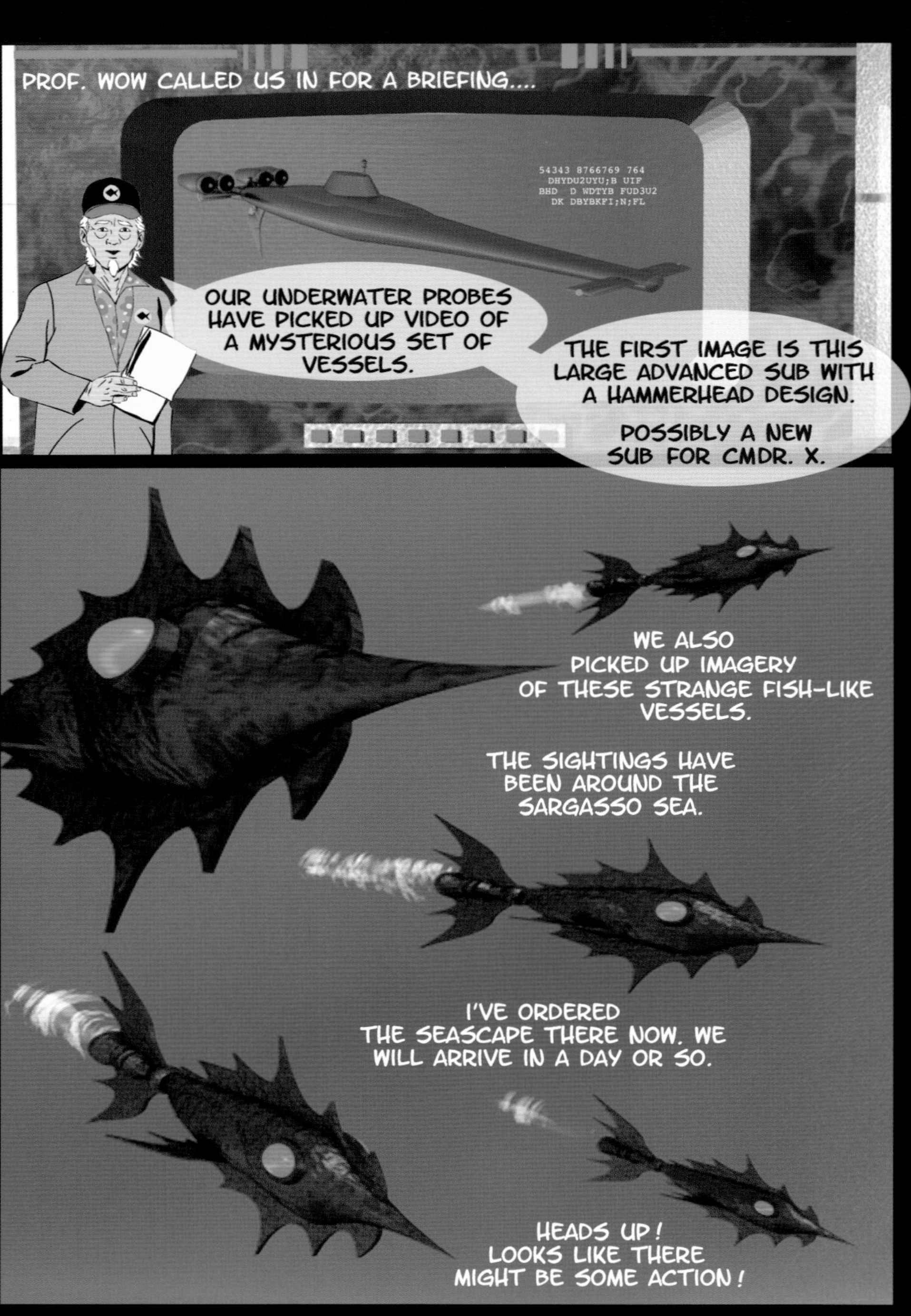
PROF. WOW CALLED US IN FOR A BRIEFING....
54343 8766769 764
DHYDU2UYU;B UIF
BHD D WDTYB FUD3U2
DK DBYBKFI;N;FL
OUR UNDERWATER PROBES HAVE PICKED UP VIDEO OF A MYSTERIOUS SET OF VESSELS.
THE FIRST IMAGE IS THIS LARGE ADVANCED SUB WITH A HAMMERHEAD DESIGN.
POSSIBLY A NEW SUB FOR CMDR. X.
WE ALSO PICKED UP IMAGERY OF THESE STRANGE FISH-LIKE VESSELS.
THE SIGHTINGS HAVE BEEN AROUND THE SARGASSO SEA.
I'VE ORDERED THE SEASCAPE THERE NOW. WE WILL ARRIVE IN A DAY OR SO.
HEADS UP! LOOKS LIKE THERE MIGHT BE SOME ACTION!

THE MYSTERY OF ME

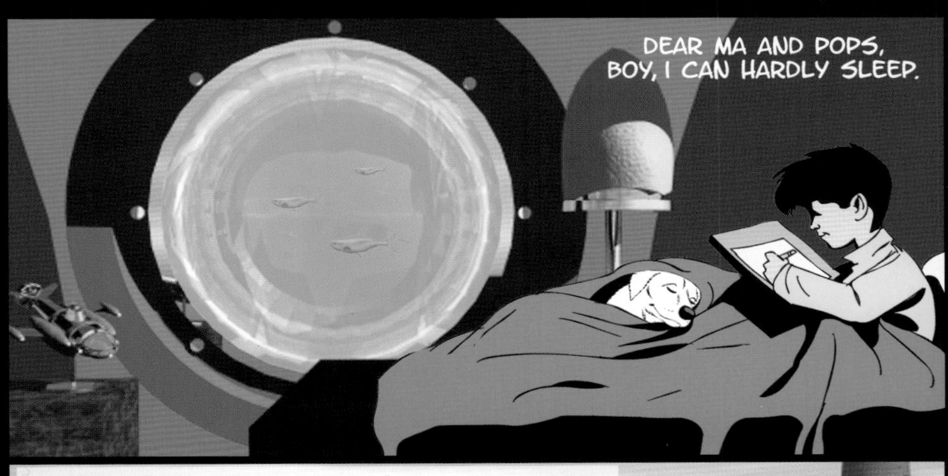

WE ARRIVE AT THE SARGASSO SEA TOMORROW AND MY FIRST MISSION AS A SEASEARCHER!

IT'S COOL BEING PART OF A TEAM, I CAN'T WAIT FOR YOU TO MEET EVERYBODY.

U.S. MAIL

I JUST WANTED TO TAKE THE TIME TO TELL YOU THAT YOU ARE RIGHT, NAVIGATING ON THE SEA IS A LOT LIKE LIFE: YOU NEVER KNOW WHAT TO EXPECT,

SO BRING A RAINCOAT.

THE MYSTERY OF ME
CONCLUDES
BUT THE STORY CONTINUES
ON THE NEXT PAGE AS
THE MYSTERY OF THE SARGASSO SEA
BEGINS....

STAND BY
FOR ADVENTURE!

THE SEA INSPIRES US TO EXPLORE.
DISCOVERY HAS ALWAYS BEEN A PART OF THE SEASEARCHERS'S MISSION.
AS THEY PLUMB THE DEPTHS, THEY ENCOUNTER UNKNOWN LIFE-FORMS-- PROVING WE ALREADY SHARE THE EARTH WITH "ALIENS."
BUT *WHO* ARE THE ALIENS?
ONE OF THE STRANGEST PLACES ON EARTH MAY HOLD THE ANSWER!
JOIN CAPT'N ELI AND THE SEASEARCHERS AS THEY UNRAVEL...
THE MYSTERY OF THE SARGASSO SEA!

THE EARTH IS TRULY AN OCEAN PLANET AND, WHEN IT COMES TO MYSTERY, IT'S A WORLD WITHOUT END!
IT'S INTERESTING THAT WE REACH TO OUTER SPACE WHEN SEVEN-TENTHS OF OUR OWN PLANET REMAINS UNEXPLORED UNDER THE SEA.
FOR CENTURIES, STRANGE AND MYSTERIOUS PLACES HAVE SPAWNED MYTHS AND LEGENDS.
SUCH A PLACE IS THE SARGASSO SEA- LOCATED IN THE HEART OF THE BERMUDA TRIANGLE.
THERE, WE'LL DISCOVER WHICH IS DEEPER: THE VAST OCEAN OR THE HUMAN IMAGINATION?

OCTOBER 31:
10 NAUTICAL MILES SOUTH OF THE SARGASSO SEA....
SOCIALITE LAWRENCE THURSTON III HAS INVITED HIS WELL-TO-DO GUESTS ABOARD HIS YACHT, THE NARCISSUS.
IT'S THE MOTHER OF ALL HALLOWEEN BASHES!
THEY ARE GOING TO TEMPT FATE
IN THE BERMUDA TRIANGLE!
AND IT SEEMS FATE IS ABOUT TO BITE ....
LOOKS LIKE BAD WEATHER.
EWW! LET'S GO INSIDE!
CAPTAIN! WE'VE ENTERED A STRANGE FOG BANK
AND THE COMPASS IS GOING CRAZY!

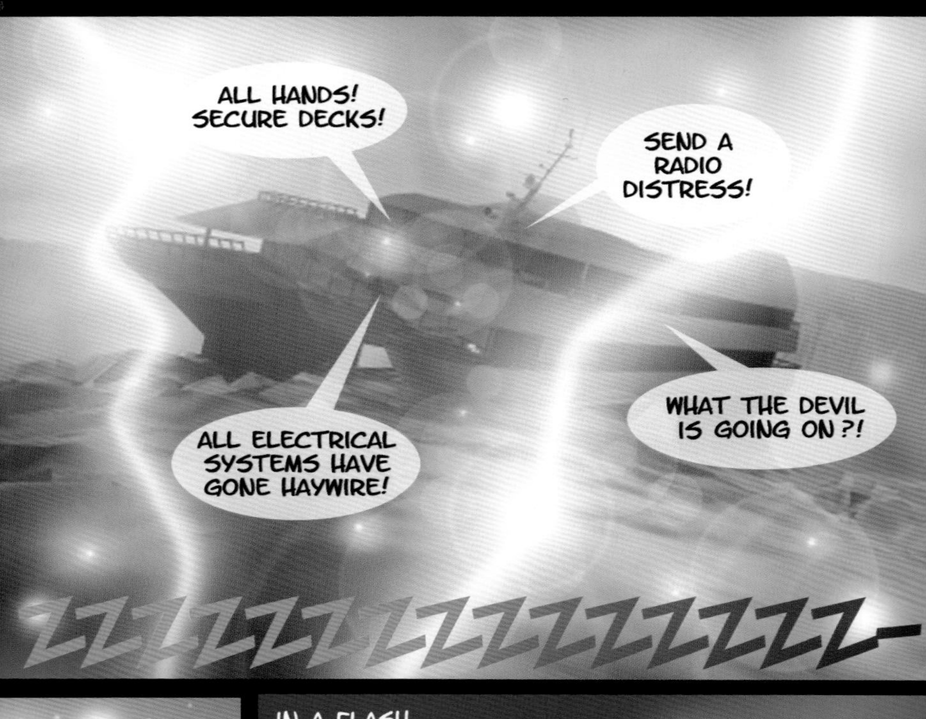
ALL HANDS! SECURE DECKS!
SEND A RADIO DISTRESS!
ALL ELECTRICAL SYSTEMS HAVE GONE HAYWIRE!
WHAT THE DEVIL IS GOING ON ?!
ZZZZZZZZZZZZZZZZ-

ZZZ-
ZATZ!

IN A FLASH...
THE NARCISSUS IS GONE!

ZZZZZZZZZZZZZZZZZZZZZZ.......
GAARROOOO!
SKREEYAH!
WHA' HAPPENED?!
WHERE ARE WE?
WHERE?
HOW ABOUT WHEN??!!
SPIELBERG!!

NOVEMBER 1:
THE MIDDLE OF THE ATLANTIC,
EAST OF THE SARGASSO SEA....
ALMOST THERE...
JUST NEED
A LITTLE MORE TIME!
SSSHHHKKKISHHHHH!!

I'VE ONLY GOT SECONDS TO MAKE IT AROUND THAT BUOY...OR... AMELIA WINS THE BET!
3
BOY! THIS ELECTRIC JET SKI CAN REALLY MOVE!
BUT THE SEA IS TOO CHOPPY...
I'M NOT GOING TO MAKE IT!!

THIS SHOULD GIVE ME AN EDGE!
CAPT'N ELI GRABS HIS NEW INVENTION,
THE ANCHOR GUN.
PSHOONT!
CLANK!
GOT IT!

THE STABILITY OF THE MAGNETIC BUOY HELPS PROPEL CAPT'N ELI.

ELI RECOUNTS HIS STUNT.

PROF. WOW STARTS THE BRIEFING.

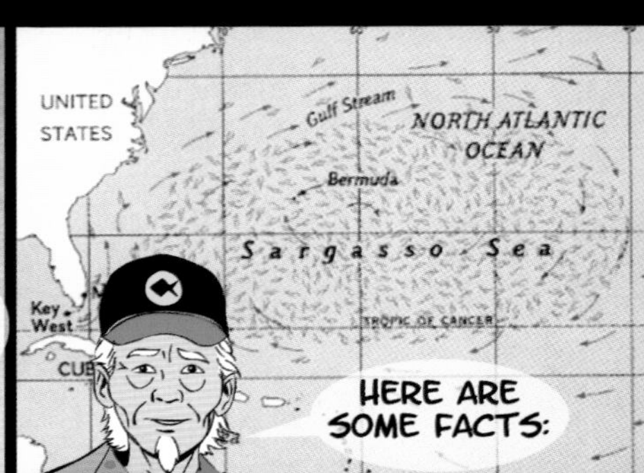

THE SARGASSO SEA OCCUPIES THAT PART OF THE ATLANTIC BETWEEN 20 DEGREES TO 35 DEGREES NORTH LATITUDE TO 30 DEGREES TO 70 DEGREES WEST LONGITUDE.

THE AREA IS CHARACTERIZED BY HUGE MATS OF SEAWEED CALLED SARGASSUM BY THE PORTUGUESE. THE SEA IS EERILY CALM, SURROUNDED BY STRONG CURRENTS.

THE FIRST RECORDS OF THE SARGASSO WERE LOGGED BY COLUMBUS.

FOOLED BY THE SEAWEED, HE THOUGHT LAND WAS NEARBY. THE SARGASSO SEA IS HUNDREDS OF MILES FROM SHORE!

HE ALSO DESCRIBED HIS COMPASS ACTING STRANGELY,

AS WELL AS THE SIGHTING OF MYSTERIOUS LIGHTS THAT FRIGHTENED HIS CREW, CAUSING A NEAR MUTINY.

IT WAS NOT THE LAST BIZARRE STORY TO COME FROM THE AREA. OVER THE YEARS, HUNDREDS OF SHIPS HAVE BEEN FOUND DERELICT OR VANISHED COMPLETELY!

EVENTUALLY THE SARGASSO SEA BECAME SHROUDED IN MYTH.

FOR YEARS, PEOPLE IMAGINED IT AS A PLACE WHERE SEAWEED CHOKED HAPLESS SHIPS, FREEZING THEM IN TIME!

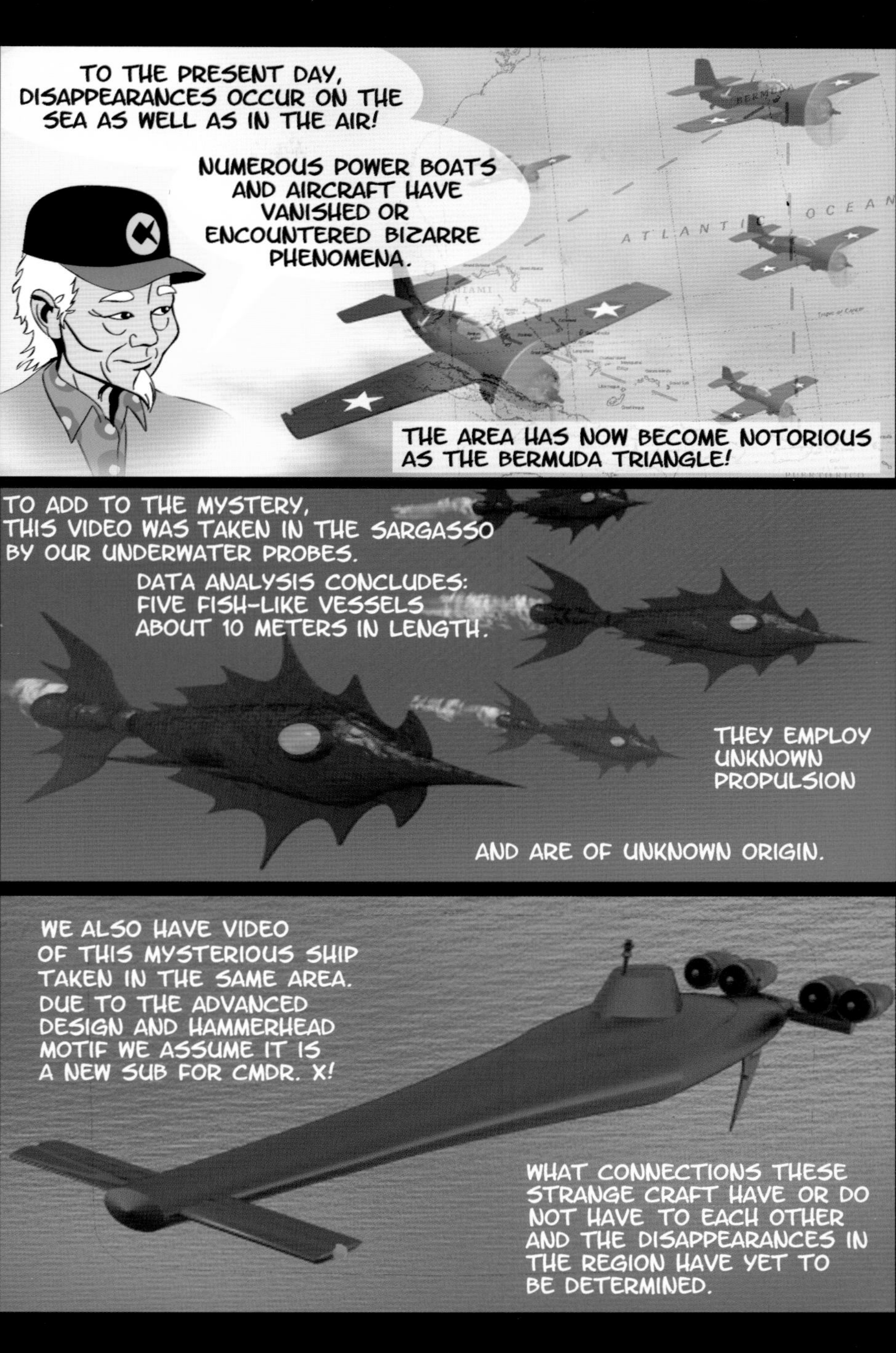

TO THE PRESENT DAY, DISAPPEARANCES OCCUR ON THE SEA AS WELL AS IN THE AIR!
NUMEROUS POWER BOATS AND AIRCRAFT HAVE VANISHED OR ENCOUNTERED BIZARRE PHENOMENA.
ATLANTIC OCEAN
MIAMI
THE AREA HAS NOW BECOME NOTORIOUS AS THE BERMUDA TRIANGLE!
TO ADD TO THE MYSTERY, THIS VIDEO WAS TAKEN IN THE SARGASSO BY OUR UNDERWATER PROBES.
DATA ANALYSIS CONCLUDES: FIVE FISH-LIKE VESSELS ABOUT 10 METERS IN LENGTH.
THEY EMPLOY UNKNOWN PROPULSION
AND ARE OF UNKNOWN ORIGIN.
WE ALSO HAVE VIDEO OF THIS MYSTERIOUS SHIP TAKEN IN THE SAME AREA. DUE TO THE ADVANCED DESIGN AND HAMMERHEAD MOTIF WE ASSUME IT IS A NEW SUB FOR CMDR. X!
WHAT CONNECTIONS THESE STRANGE CRAFT HAVE OR DO NOT HAVE TO EACH OTHER AND THE DISAPPEARANCES IN THE REGION HAVE YET TO BE DETERMINED.

PROF. WOW, DUE TO THE DANGEROUS NATURE OF OUR DESTINATION AND THE UNPREDICTABLE CMDR. X,
I SUGGEST ELI MIGHT NOT BE QUALIFIED FOR THIS MISSION.
I UNDERSTAND, CMDR. BUT OUR YOUNG CAPT'N IS ONE OF THE ONLY PEOPLE ALIVE TO MAKE CONTACT WITH CMDR. X!
ELI, MAYBE YOU CAN SHARE YOUR INSIGHTS?
SURE! I THINK CMDR. X IS OK! A LITTLE LOUD, BUT OK!
AS YOU KNOW, I MET HIM RESCUING A U.S. SUB.
AFTER LOCATING THE SUB, I HAD SOME TROUBLE GETTING IT TO THE SURFACE.
CMDR. X APPEARED FROM NOWHERE AND SAVED THE DAY!
I THANKED HIM AND HE SAID WE WOULD MEET AGAIN!
HOW'S THAT FOR QUALIFIED, "HORATIO HORNBLOWER?!"
EASY, ROGER, JUST DOING MY JOB. I CONCEDE ELI IS A VALUABLE TEAMMATE.
BUT, AS SECURITY CHIEF, I EXPECT YOU TO FOLLOW SAFETY PROTOCOL TO THE LETTER!
CHECK, COMMANDER! BY THE WAY, DO YOU KNOW WHO CMDR. X REALLY IS?

ACT I - THE MYSTERY OF THE SARGASSO SEA

COMMANDER X IS STILL AS MUCH OF A MYSTERY AS HE WAS OVER 60 YEARS AGO!

BESIDES THE RUMORS, THIS IS WHAT WE KNOW:

IN THE GOLDEN AGE OF THE ULTRA-HEROES AND MYSTERY MEN, CMDR. X WAS ONE OF THE GREATEST.

HE CAME FROM NOWHERE, FIGHTING WITH THE ALLIES IN WWII.

HE VOWED TO BATTLE EVIL, USING ADVANCED WEAPONRY AND THE AMAZING SUB X!

HIS EXPLOITS BECAME SO FAMOUS THAT HE WAS FICTIONALIZED IN RADIO PLAYS, COMIC BOOKS AND MOVIE SERIALS.

SEA WAR COMICS
STARRING... COMMANDER X

HE WAS THE LEADER OF AN ULTRA-TEAM CALLED "THE BIG 3."

HIS OTHER TEAMMATES WERE:

THE SAVAGE SEA RAIDER AND THE RADIOACTIVE HUMAN SUN.

AFTER THE WAR WAS WON, COMMANDER X DISAPPEARED, LIKE SO MANY OTHER LOST HEROES.

HE RESURFACED A FEW YEARS AGO- ENGAGING IN A PRIVATE WAR WITH THE "SURFACE WORLD," AS HE CALLS IT.

SPARING THEIR CREWS, CMDR. X SINKS SHIPS FOR REASONS OF HIS OWN.

DESPITE YOUR SUB RESCUE, ELI, THE WORLD SEES CMDR. X AS A RENEGADE!

OKEY DOKEY!
LET ME GET THIS STRAIGHT.
OUR MISSION IS: RESCUE A MISSING YACHT, POSSIBLY CONTEND WITH ALIEN SUBS AND A SUB-SEA ZORRO!
ALL THIS AND A WISECRACKING PARROT IN THE MIDDLE OF THE BERMUDA TRIANGLE!
PHEW!
HEY, I'M JUST TRYING TO ADD A LITTLE ZING, LIKE HOT SAUCE!
BE GLAD BARNEY CAN'T TALK!
ARF!
SOUNDS GOOD!
I SUPPOSE WE HAVE A PLAN?
YES, WELL, WE DO HAVE A PLAN! LET ME PASS THE BRIEFING TO DR. BOLO AND SHE CAN FILL US IN.
DR. BOLO?

THANK YOU, PROF. WOW.
LET ME INTRODUCE YOU TO SOMETHING WE'VE BEEN WORKING ON: THE ANTI-MATTER TRANSMITTER, OR ANTI-M!
ANTI-M WILL ASSIST OUR MISSION IN THREE WAYS:
#1. PROTECT OUR CRAFT BY DAMPENING ELECTRO-MAGNETIC DISTURBANCE.
#2. DETECT ELECTRO-MAGNETIC ANOMALIES.
#3. DEPLOY A HOMING BEACON.
ANTI-M IS NOW STANDARD ISSUE IN YOUR VEHICLES AND EQUIPMENT.
OUR PLAN IS TO EMPLOY ANTI-M IN A STANDARD SEARCH PATTERN.
PROF. WOW AND RED WILL MONITOR IN THE SEASCAPE.
I WILL PILOT THE HYDRO-COPTER AND OBSERVE BY AIR.
CAPT'N ELI AND THE DOLPHIN WILL BE ATTACHED TO A RETRACTABLE TETHER
AND TAKE READINGS BELOW THE SURFACE.
CMDR. FATHOM AND THE TRIDENT WILL BE ON STAND-BY, READY FOR ANY TROUBLE.
LOOKS LIKE I'M GOING TO BE BAIT.
BASICALLY, WE ALL ARE. I'M REELING YOU IN IF TROUBLE ARISES!
WELL, THAT'S IT!
IF THERE ARE NO MORE COMMENTS OR QUESTIONS, THEN...
SEASEARCHERS, TO YOUR POSTS!
GOOD LUCK, AND BE CAREFUL OUT THERE!

THE MISSION BEGINS IN THE SEASCAPE'S OPERATIONS ROOM....

SEASCAPE TO HYDROCOPTER AND DOLPHIN,

BEGIN SCAN OF AREA 1.

COPY? – OVER.

HYDROCOPTER TO SEASCAPE,

I COPY, SCANNING INITIATED.

THE AIR IS THICK AND MOTIONLESS...

NO WONDER SAILING SHIPS DREADED THIS PLACE! -OVER.

DOLPHIN TO SEASCAPE. COPY, I'M SCANNING!

THIS IS AMAZING! ABOVE ME ARE THE HUGE MATS OF SARGASSUM AND BELOW IS SOME KIND OF LUMINOUS ALGAE! -OVER.

SEASCAPE TO HYDROCOPTER AND DOLPHIN, COPY YOUR OBSERVATIONS, NOTHING UNUSUAL FOR THE AREA. -OVER.

GRID AREA 12, CLEAR.
MOVING ON TO GRID AREA 13, -OVER.
HOURS PASS....
DOLPHIN TO SEASCAPE, GRID AREA 30 CLEAR!
I HOPE WE GOT A PLAN B!
THIS DOESN'T SEEM TO BE WORKING,-OVER.
LOOKS LIKE WE MIGHT NEED PLAN B.
HYDROCOPTER TO SEASCAPE, ALERT!
THE ANTI-M TRANSMITTER IS GOING WILD!

SEASCAPE, WE HAVE A PROBLEM!
END OF ACT 1

Act 2

Into The Vortex

AMELIA ENCOUNTERS AN IRRESISTIBLE FORCE....
...ANOMALY...
...SEASCAPE, DO YOU READ?...
...CAN'T...
...BEING DRAWN IN!...
SEASCAPE TO HYDROCOPTER, AMELIA, YOU'RE BREAKING UP...
TRY ANOTHER FREQUENCY, RED.
AMELIA, THIS IS HAJEME. ABORT MISSION, RETURN TO BASE...
WE'RE LOSING RADAR CONTACT!
PROFESSOR, YOU'RE NOT GOING TO BELIEVE THIS! THE DOLPHIN HAS BROKEN FROM ITS TETHER!
POIT!
HANG ON, AMELIA...
I'M ON MY WAY!

ACT 2 - INTO THE VORTEX

I'M GOING IN!

THE DOLPHIN ENTERS ANOTHER DIMENSION.

ACT 2 - INTO THE VORTEX

"AN ENTRANCE CAN BE AN EXIT." -GAROO

CAPT'N ELI TRIES TO GET HIS BEARINGS....

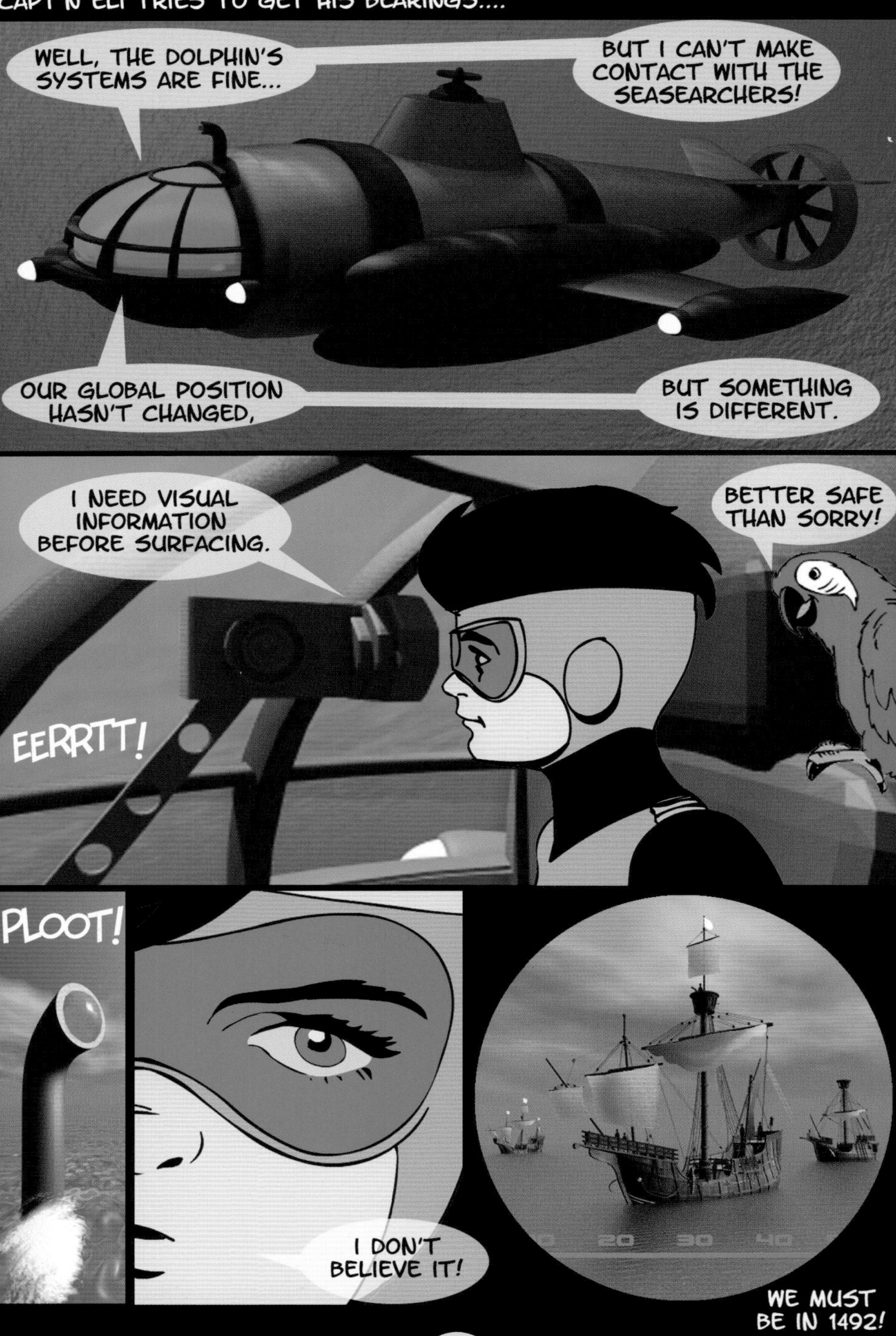

Act 2 - Into the Vortex

ROGER TAKES A LOOK....

WELL, YEARS AGO I WAS FREELANCING

ABOARD THE RUDDY ROSE WITH CAPT. JACK SCURVEY. ONE NIGHT IN THE SARGASSO WE SAILED INTO A PINK CLOUD!

WE ALL FELL FAST ASLEEP. THE NEXT MORNING WE ARRIVED IN PORT.

AN ENTIRE WEEK HAD PASSED AND WE HAD NO MEMORY OF IT! THAT WAS A WEIRD TIME!

TIME IS THE ANSWER! WE'VE TRAVELED THROUGH A TIME VORTEX! BUT THIS DISCOVERY BEGS MORE QUESTIONS THAN IT ANSWERS!

YEAH... LIKE, HOW DO WE GET HOME?

I DON'T KNOW, ROGER,

THE MYSTERY OF THE SARGASSO SEA

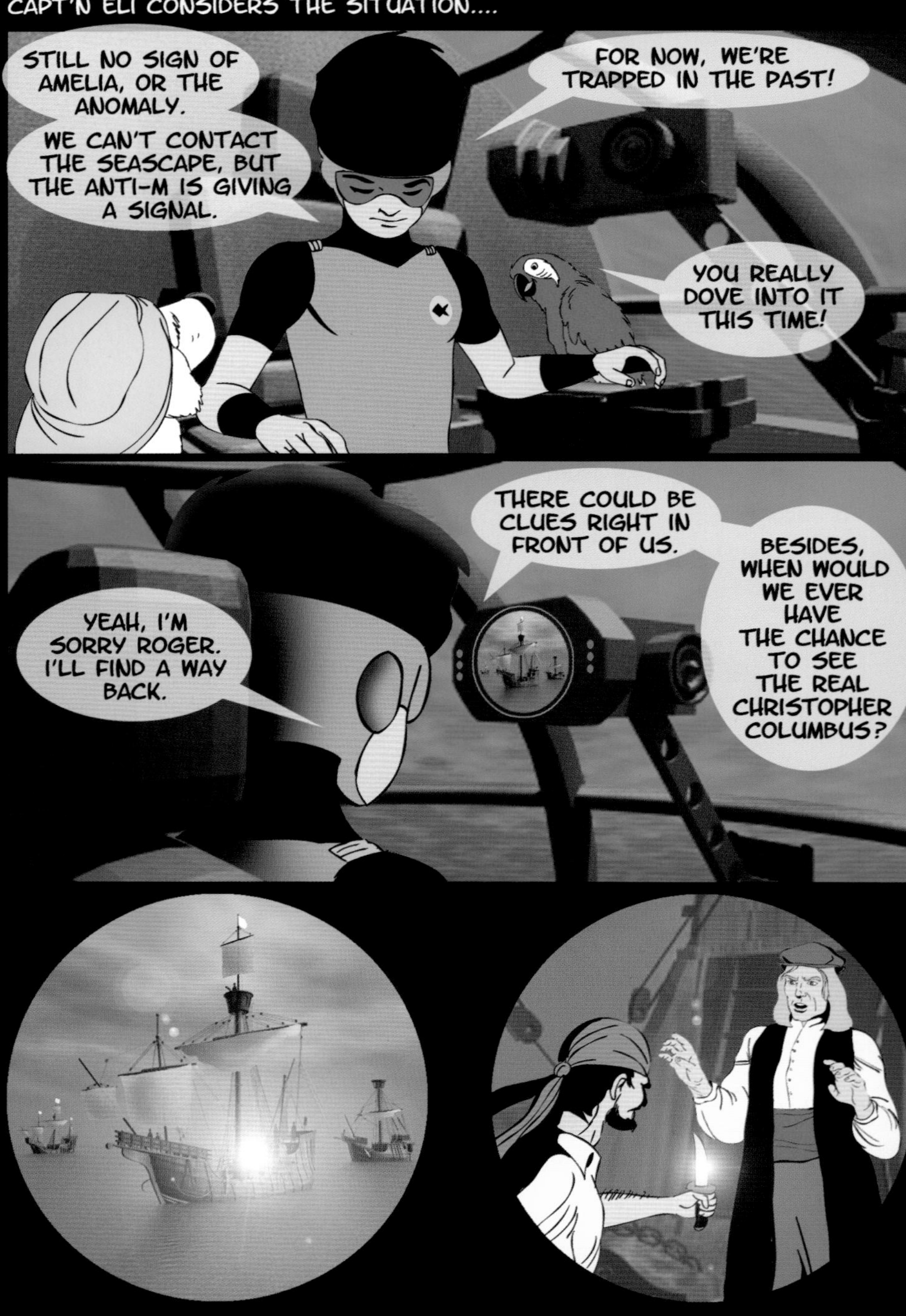

ACT 2 - INTO THE VORTEX

WORMHOLE? LIKE A BLACK HOLE?
BUT HOW? AREN'T WORMHOLES OUTER SPACE PHENOMENA?
I'M NOT SURE HOW, RED, BUT I'M GOING TO FIND OUT!
I KNOW IT SOUNDS IMPOSSIBLE, BUT I THINK OUR FRIENDS HAVE TRAVELLED IN TIME, NOT SPACE.
OBSERVE THIS HOLOGRAM. THE RED DOTS ARE AMELIA AND ELI'S ANTI-M SIGNALS.
THE ANTI-M SIGNAL IS STILL BEING BROADCAST ALTHOUGH THEY APPEAR TO HAVE VANISHED.
WE CAN'T SEE THEM, BUT THEY ARE HERE, IN THE FOURTH DIMENSION--TIME!
THE SIGNALS ARE WEAKER THAN NORMAL. IF I CAN CALCULATE THE SIGNAL STRENGTH COMPARED TO THE ANTI-M'S HALF-LIFE I MIGHT BE ABLE TO FIND "WHEN" THEY ARE.
THEN WE CAN USE THE ANTI-M TO FIND THE RIGHT FREQUENCY AND MAKE RADIO CONTACT!

ACT 2 - INTO THE VORTEX

WE RETURN TO THE MUTINY, ALREADY IN PROGRESS....

ROGER TRANSLATES FOR ELI.

ELI, THIS BOTHERS ME ON SO MANY LEVELS...
I DON'T HAVE TIME TO FIND OUT WHAT YOU'RE DOING...
BUT I NEED YOU TO GET BACK TO THE DOLPHIN, NOW!
WE'VE GOT AN EMERGENCY!
EMERGENCY? BESIDES BEING TRAPPED IN THE PAST?
SHE SOUNDS SERIOUS.
NO TIME TO EXPLAIN!
MOVE!
BARNEY, BRING UP THE DOLPHIN.
ARF!

WELL, IT'S BEEN FUN, BUT WE GOTTA GO! REMEMBER, LAND IS WITHIN YOUR REACH! GOODBYE, CAPTAIN!
GRAB THE BOY!
HE TALKS TO THE BIRD AND HIS HAND!
AND THEY TALK BACK!
LET'S FLY!
NO PROBLEMO!
SOON....
OK, AMELIA, WHAT'S UP?
ELI, OUR SITUATION HAS BECOME WORSE...

CHECK YOUR RADAR SCANNER.

SCANNING...

WHAT?! IT CAN'T BE! A FLEET OF SUBS HEADING THIS WAY!

THEY'RE THE FISH-LIKE SUBS WE'VE BEEN LOOKING FOR.
COMING IN FAST, E.T.A. THREE MINUTES.

GEE, AMELIA! WHAT DO YOU THINK THEY WANT?

I TRIED TO MAKE RADIO CONTACT EARLIER. THEY CAN'T OR WON'T RESPOND.
THEIR SPEED AND NUMBER TELLS ME THEY ARE AGGRESSIVE!
WHO DO THEY WANT, US OR COLUMBUS?
I HAVE NO IDEA...
BUT I DO KNOW THIS...
WE NEED A PLAN...
NOW!

ELI GETS AN IDEA....

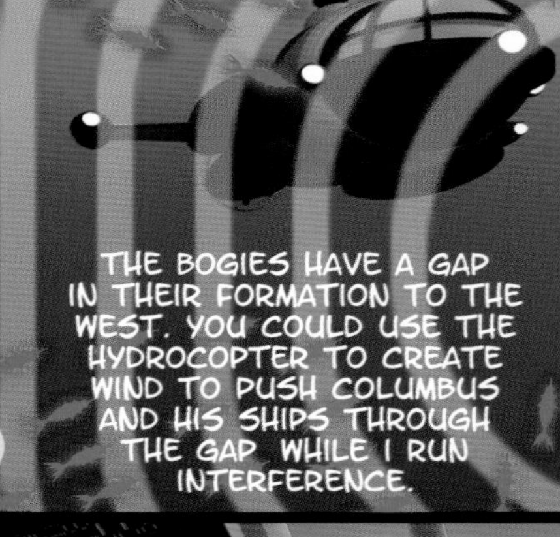

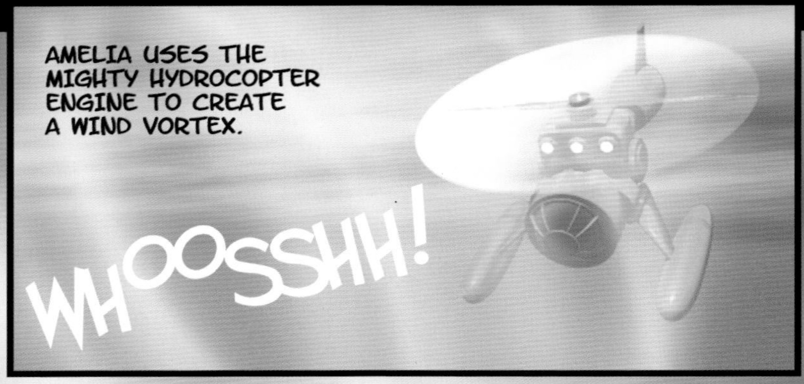
AMELIA USES THE MIGHTY HYDROCOPTER ENGINE TO CREATE A WIND VORTEX.
WHOOSSHH!

IT'S WORKING!
THE WIND! SHE IS BACK!

Act 2 - Into the Vortex

AMELIA "PUSHES" COLUMBUS ON COURSE.

ALMOST THERE! HOW ARE YOU DOING, ELI?

I'M IN RANGE, AMELIA...

I'VE MADE VISUAL CONTACT! WHOA! THERE MUST BE THOUSANDS OF 'EM!

FIRST WAVE COMIN' IN...

HANG ON!

THE MYSTERIOUS SUBS ATTACK...

SHOOM!

FRAFFLE! THESE BOGIES MEAN BUSINESS!

SHOOM!

CHA-CHOOM!
WE'RE HIT!
TWO MORE COMING IN HOT AND FAST!
ZAZATZZ!
HAVE NO FEAR!
THEY'RE CALLED HYDRONS! I'M MORE THAN A MATCH FOR THEM!
COMMANDER X HAS RETURNED!

END OF ACT 2

Act 3

The Mysterious Commander X

ACT 3 - THE MYSTERIOUS COMMANDER X

BACK IN 1492....
FOR BETTER OR WORSE, HISTORY IS ON TRACK AND COLUMBUS IS ON HIS WAY.
NOW TO GET BACK TO ELI!
SEASCAPE TO HYDROCOPTER, DO YOU READ? - OVER.
HAJEME!
I READ YOU! BUT HOW?
WE FOUND YOU WITH THE ANTI-M DEVICE!
WE ARE WORKING ON A WAY TO BRING YOU BACK!
AMELIA, WHAT IS YOUR SITUATION?

IT'S NOT GOOD!
WE'RE OUTNUMBERED AND UNDER ATTACK BY THE FISH-LIKE SUBS!

WE'RE TRYING TO PREVENT THEM FROM TAMPERING WITH HISTORY!

ELI HAS ENGAGED THE HOSTILES...
CHISH-KA-

CHOOM!
I'M GOING IN TO HELP HIM NOW!

THE MYSTERY OF THE SARGASSO SEA

THE BATTLE CONTINUES....

ELI MOVES INTO POSITION...
TWO GIANT DOORS UNDER CMDR. X'S SUB SLIDE OPEN...
ELI, STOP YOUR ENGINE. MY TRACTOR BEAM IS TAKING CONTROL!
AND THE DOLPHIN RISES INSIDE.
ALL SECURE!
ENGAGE ANTI-MATTER WAVE!
ZZAT-ZZZZZZZ!!
A SHELL OF ENERGY SURROUNDS THE SUB.

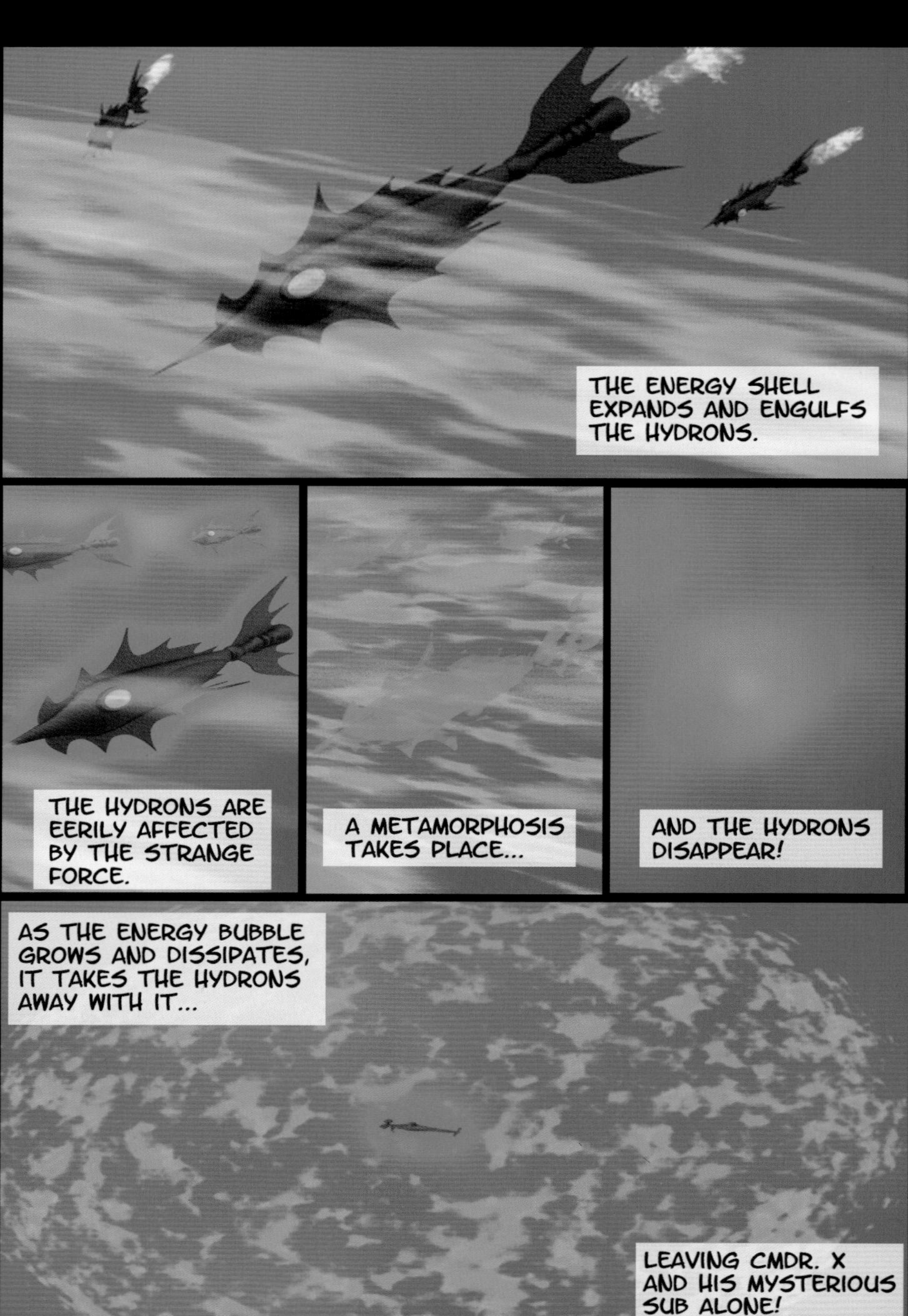
THE ENERGY SHELL EXPANDS AND ENGULFS THE HYDRONS.
THE HYDRONS ARE EERILY AFFECTED BY THE STRANGE FORCE.
A METAMORPHOSIS TAKES PLACE...
AND THE HYDRONS DISAPPEAR!
AS THE ENERGY BUBBLE GROWS AND DISSIPATES, IT TAKES THE HYDRONS AWAY WITH IT...
LEAVING CMDR. X AND HIS MYSTERIOUS SUB ALONE!

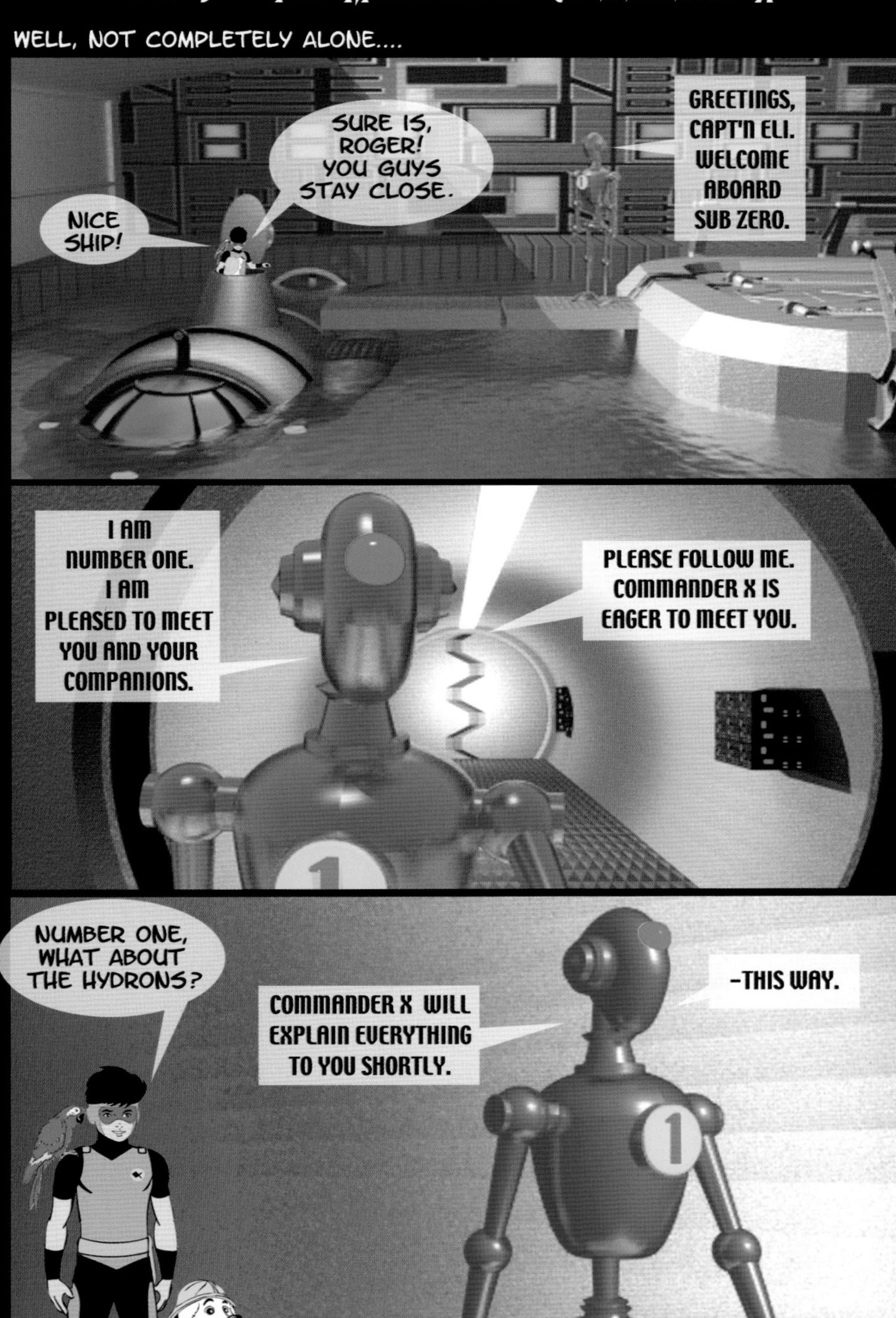
WELL, NOT COMPLETELY ALONE....
NICE SHIP!
SURE IS, ROGER! YOU GUYS STAY CLOSE.
GREETINGS, CAPT'N ELI. WELCOME ABOARD SUB ZERO.
I AM NUMBER ONE. I AM PLEASED TO MEET YOU AND YOUR COMPANIONS.
PLEASE FOLLOW ME. COMMANDER X IS EAGER TO MEET YOU.
NUMBER ONE, WHAT ABOUT THE HYDRONS?
COMMANDER X WILL EXPLAIN EVERYTHING TO YOU SHORTLY.
-THIS WAY.

SHORTLY....
THIS IS THE BRIDGE.
COMMANDER X IS BEHIND THESE DOORS.
"THE MAN BEHIND THE CURTAIN."
RIGHT! WIZARD OF OZ! NOW, BEHAVE!
SIR, YOUR GUESTS HAVE ARRIVED.
THANK YOU, NUMBER ONE.
IT IS GOOD TO MEET YOU FACE TO FACE, ELI.
I'M SURE YOU HAVE MANY QUESTIONS.

AMELIA ARRIVES ON THE SCENE....
ELI'S ANTI-M SIGNAL HAS FAILED!
HE AND THE FISH SUBS ARE GONE!
AND THIS OMINOUS SUB REMAINS!
HAILING UNKNOWN SUB!
THIS IS DR. AMELIA BOLO!
I WARN YOU, IF MY TEAMMATE HAS BEEN HARMED YOU WILL BE BROUGHT TO JUSTICE!
DR. BOLO!
I'M A FAN OF YOUR WORK!
THIS IS COMMANDER X!
YOUR TEAMMATE IS SAFE.
AND SO ARE YOU.
FAZATZ!
BON VOYAGE.

THE HYDROCOPTER IS AFFECTED IN A SIMILAR FASHION AS THE HYDRONS...
AND DISAPPEARS!
POP!
AMELIA!
FRAFFLE! YOU BETTER NOT HAVE HURT HER!
THEY TOLD ME YOU WERE A VILLAIN...
WHEN YOU PULL A STUNT LIKE THAT, I BELIEVE 'EM!
YOU TELL 'IM KID!
GRRR!
I'M SORRY MY ACTIONS STARTLED YOU...
DR. BOLO HAS BEEN SAFELY RETURNED TO THE PRESENT.
SOON WE WILL FOLLOW.
THE HYDRONS ARE BACK WHERE THEY BELONG AS WELL.
REGARDLESS OF WHAT YOU HAVE BEEN TOLD, ELI,
I HAVE VOWED NEVER TO KILL.

ACT 3 - THE MYSTERIOUS COMMANDER X

YES, THERE IS MUCH TO LEARN. YOU'LL NEED TIME TO GET UP TO SPEED.
YOU CAN BE BRIEFED WHILE YOUR SUB IS BEING REPAIRED HERE ON SUB ZERO.
WHAT ABOUT MY FRIENDS?
THEY'RE GOING TO BE WORRIED IF I DON'T CHECK IN.

WE WILL RETURN TO OUR OWN TIME NOW.
YOU CAN MAKE CONTACT WITH YOUR TEAM.
IF THERE ARE ANY OBJECTIONS TO YOU STAYING ABOARD, YOU MAY LEAVE.

SOUNDS REASONABLE! LET'S GO!
IT'S ABOUT TIME!

ENGAGE ANTI-MATTER WAVE!
ZZAZZATZZ!

ACT 3 - THE MYSTERIOUS COMMANDER X

MEANWHILE, BACK IN THE PRESENT....

ELI RELAYS AN AMAZING STORY....
CMDR. X SAYS THE TIME WARP IS GONE FOR NOW.
IN TIME, HE SAYS HE WILL EXPLAIN EVERYTHING!
SO CAN I STAY?
WELL, THIS IS ALL A BIT MUCH! BUT, IF YOU MAKE CONTACT AT REGULAR INTERVALS, I DON'T SEE A PROBLEM.
GOOD LUCK. WE'LL TALK SOON, ELI!
OVER AND OUT!
WHAT?! ARE YOU SURE THIS IS A PRUDENT COURSE OF ACTION? WHAT IF CMDR. X IS JUST USING ELI FOR SOME KIND OF DECEPTION?
I DON'T THINK SO, MARK. I'M WILLING TO GIVE CMDR. X THE BENEFIT OF THE DOUBT.
SO FAR CMDR. X'S ACTIONS HAVE BEEN BENEVOLENT. HE RECOVERED OUR TEAMMATES AND DID OUR JOB FINDING THE NARCISSUS.
TO BE HONEST, I FEEL THERE IS A CONNECTION BETWEEN ELI AND THE COMMANDER.
WHILE CMDR. X HOLDS ALL THE CARDS, ELI MIGHT HELP SHED LIGHT ON THE SITUATION.
NOW, LET'S GO GIVE AMELIA A HAND!

ACT 3 - THE MYSTERIOUS COMMANDER X

...AND THIS SHIP.

THE SUB'S AUTO-PILOT KICKED IN AND LANDED US ON THE BOTTOM OF THE SEA.

I TRIED TO ACCESS INFORMATION ABOUT MY IDENTITY FROM THE SUB'S COMPUTER.

I FAILED. THE COMPUTER WAS JUST LIKE MY BRAIN, ALL OF ITS TECHNICAL FUNCTIONS INTACT, BUT ITS MEMORY FILES AND LOGS WERE ERASED!

EXCEPT ONE:

A FILE MARKED "SHIVA."

IN MYTHOLOGY, SHIVA IS THE GOD OF DESTRUCTION AND CREATION.

THE FILE DESCRIBED A BLEAK FUTURE. THE WHOLE WORLD WAS DELUGED. CONTINENTS AND CIVILIZATIONS DISAPPEARED!

THE EARTH WAS A WORLD OF WATER!

THE FILE ALSO HAD A WAY TO STOP THIS CATASTROPHE.

A LIST OF SPECIAL MISSIONS, EACH WITH DATES, NAMES AND LOCATIONS. IF EACH MISSION WAS COMPLETED, THE COURSE OF HISTORY WOULD CHANGE AND THE WORLD WOULD BE SAVED!

ACT 3 - THE MYSTERIOUS COMMANDER X

THESE WERE THE WORST OF TIMES AND THE BEST. AS MY ADVENTURES GREW, I MADE SOME FRIENDS. THAT'S WHEN I KNEW BISCUIT. MY COMRADES WERE VERY SPECIAL TO ME. THEY HELPED ME COMPLETE SOME OF MY MOST DIFFICULT MISSIONS, YET NEVER KNEW ABOUT THE SHIVA LIST. I SHARED THE SECRET ONLY WITH MY FELLOW ULTRA-HEROES...

I REVEALED MY SECRET TO THE ULTRA-HEROES
BECAUSE WE SHARED A COMMON ENEMY
AND THEY ARE ON THE SHIVA LIST --
THE HYDRONS!
THE HYDRONS ARE THE ARCH ENEMY OF THE SEA RAIDER,
WHO, IN TIME, BECAME THE SEA GHOST!
NOW, HE IS AQUARIUS, THE RULER OF HIS OWN UNDERSEA KINGDOM!
FRAFFLE! AN UNDERSEA KINGDOM?!
HEY, I ALWAYS WANTED TO SEE ONE OF THOSE!
WELL, NOW IS YOUR CHANCE! I THOUGHT THE BEST PLACE TO FINISH YOUR BRIEFING IS HERE.

WELCOME TO AQUARIA!

SOMEWHERE DEEP IN THE BOWELS OF THE EARTH....

END OF ACT 3

TO BE CONTINUED.....

Stand by for adventure as Commander X shows Capt'n Eli, Barney, and Roger the wonders and dangers of the undersea kingdom of Aquaria. Ask for *The Undersea Adventures of Capt'n Eli: Volume 2* at your favorite store or visit us at www.captneli.com!
But for now, turn the page and check out a story
FROM THE VAULT
and relive the Golden Age of comics with Commander X.

A Capt'n Eli Publication
THE BIG 3 COMICS
10¢
STAND BY FOR ADVENTURE!
Featuring...
COMMANDER X
SEA RAIDER
and
HUMAN SUN

SEA RAIDER
COMMANDER X
HUMAN SUN
THE BIG 3
IN
THE RETURN OF BARON HYDRO

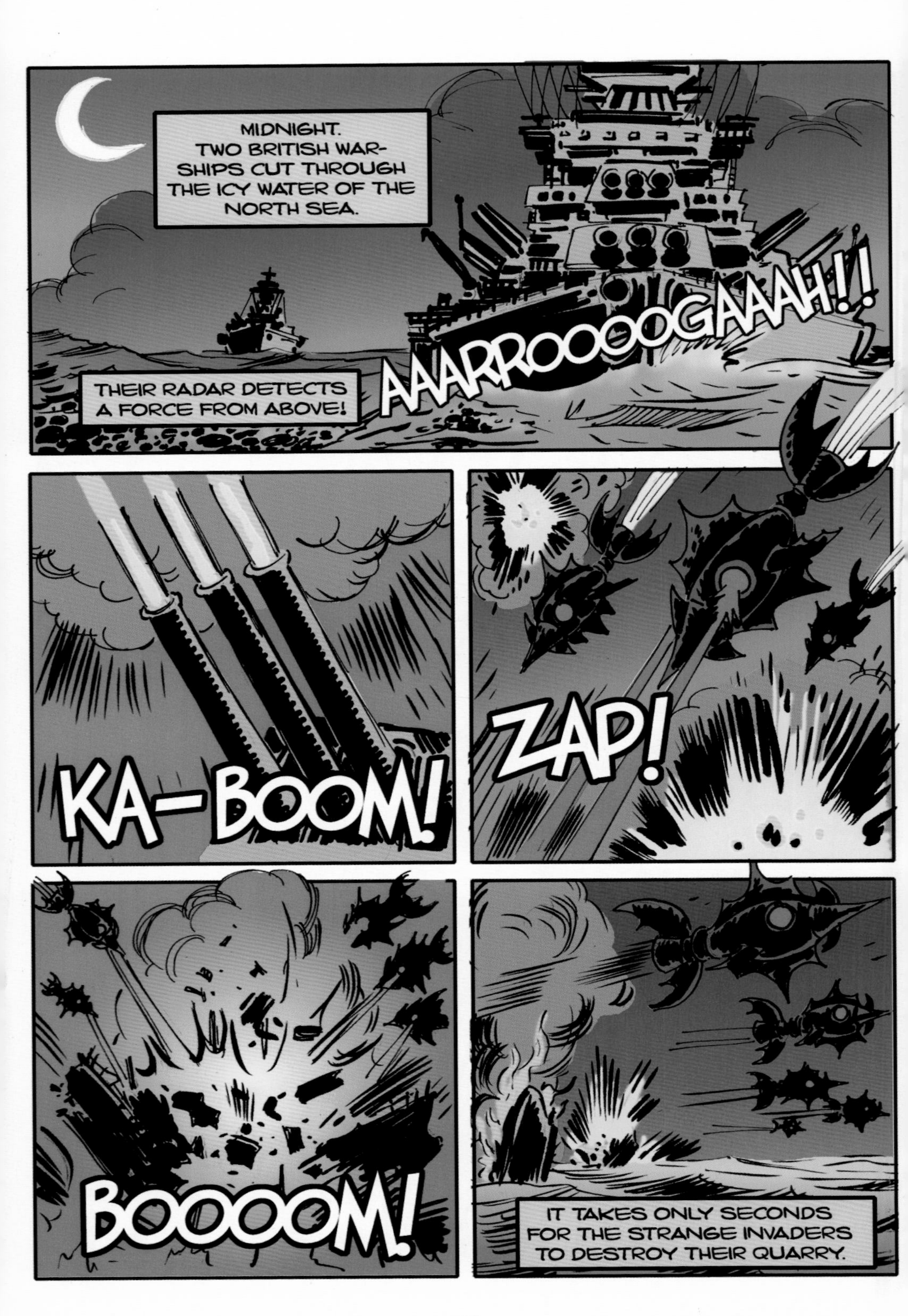
MIDNIGHT.
TWO BRITISH WAR-SHIPS CUT THROUGH THE ICY WATER OF THE NORTH SEA.
THEIR RADAR DETECTS A FORCE FROM ABOVE!
AAARROOOOGAAAH!!
KA-BOOM!
ZAP!
BOOOOM!
IT TAKES ONLY SECONDS FOR THE STRANGE INVADERS TO DESTROY THEIR QUARRY.

WASHINGTON, D.C.
TRIPLE SECRET ULTRA FORCE H.Q. GEN. T.F. MCGRAW IN COMMAND.
THE INTREPID AND THE HORNET WERE FINE SHIPS...
SO WERE THEIR CREWS.
BARON HYDRO AND HIS HYDRONS!
INDEED! HONOR DEMANDS I MUST FIGHT HIM ALONE!
NOT THIS AGAIN!

LUCKILY, THERE ARE SURVIVORS. THEY EYEWITNESSED FLYING FISH-SHIPS!

THIS ISN'T THE TIME FOR PERSONAL FEUDS, RAIDER, THIS IS WAR!
THE HIGH COMMAND ORDERS THE BIG 3, THAT'S ALL OF YOU, TO STOP THIS MANIAC, CLEAR?!

A.O.K., SIR!
WE'RE ALL IN THIS TOGETHER, AMIGO!
THANKS, X.

THIS AIN'T NO COMMUNITY SING! GET MOVIN'! FALL OUT!
BIG 3, LET'S GO!

A FEW DAYS LATER IN THE NORTH SEA...
ONCE AGAIN, AN ALLIED SHIP FALLS PREY....

TO VERY STRANGE PREDATORS!

IN THE WINK OF AN EYE, THE HAPLESS SHIP DISAPPEARS! IT WAS BUT AN ILLUSION! THE SURPRISED HYDRONS ARE CAUGHT DUMBFOUNDED!

WHOOOSH!!
PEEK-A-BOO!

WE'VE GOT THE JUMP ON 'EM!
THANKS TO THE THREE-DIMENSIONAL TELEVISION PROJECTOR!
YOU'VE GOT BRAINS, X! BUT NOW IT'S TIME FOR SOME BRAWN!
WHAM!
WHAT MAKES YOU THINK YOU HAVE EITHER, FISH-MAN?
BAM!
YOU'RE GONNA FIND OUT, FIRE-BUG!
ZAP!
COOL DOWN, YOU TWO! SAVE IT FOR THE HYDRONS!

THE HYDRONS SPRING FROM THEIR BROKEN SHIPS!
CRASH!
NOT TODAY, HYDRON!
SOCKO!
THEY'RE NOTHING BUT MINDLESS EELS!
THUD!
WHOOSH!
HOW ABOUT A FISH FRY?
SPLASH!

GOOD JOB! WE'VE GOT 'EM ON THE RUN!

WE CAN TRACK THEM TO BARON HYDRO!
FOLLOW ME IN SUB X!

NOT SO FAST, RAIDER! I'M RIGHT HERE!
LOOKS LIKE HYDRO'S GOT A PROJECTOR GIZMO, TOO!
YES, BUT THE SIGNAL IS LIMITED. HE MUST BE CLOSE BY.
HYDRO!
WRONG! I'M BROADCASTING FROM A SECRET BASE FAR AWAY!
MY AQUARIAN SCIENCE IS MORE THAN A MATCH FOR YOUR FUTURISTIC TOYS!
I SHALL TAUNT YOU FROM AFAR AS I SEIZE CONTROL OF THE WORLD!

I AM THE FULFILLMENT OF THE ANCIENT PROPHECY! ONCE THE SURFACE WORLD IS CRUSHED, I WILL CLAIM AQUARIA AS ITS KING!

WELL, I PREDICT YOU WON'T GET VERY FAR!
YOU ARE A COWARD, HYDRO!
WE'LL FIND A WAY TO ROUT YOU OUT!

COWARD, EH! YOU'LL EAT YOUR WORDS WHEN YOU SEE MY NEXT TARGET! I'LL EVEN GIVE YOU A CLUE....ZZZZZZZZZZZ!

WHAT ARE YOU DOING? HE WAS GOING TO REVEAL HIS PLANS!
HE'S GIVEN UP MORE THAN THAT....
EVERY SIGNAL CAN BE TRACED TO ITS SOURCE! C'MON!

USING HIS FUTURISTIC GADGETRY, CMDR. X TRACES BARON HYDRO'S SIGNAL TO A SUNKEN RUIN OF ATLANTIS.

GUEST ARTIST GALLERY

I am grateful to have contributions by these legendary creators. Each has been a major influence on my work and *The Undersea Adventures of Capt'n Eli.*

STEVE RUDE is one of the most honored illustrators in the comic book field, and he deserves it! The world first got to see Steve's work in the 80's when he pioneered NEXUS with writer Mike Baron. Since then, he has created for every major company and brought NEXUS back to print in 2007. Steve continues to blaze the trail with Rude Dude Productions which publishes NEXUS as well as his own creation the MOTH. He is also the author of *Steve Rude: Artist in Motion* which shares his artistic process and vision. www.steverude.com

HERB TRIMPE is famous for defining the look of the Hulk for Marvel in the 70's. His versatile, fun style has graced practically all the Marvel heroes. My personal favorites are The Phantom Eagle and Shogun Warriors. In addition to being a comic book legend, Herb is a teacher, author and an ordained deacon. His book, *The Power of Angels,* chronicles his experiences at Ground Zero during the period following the 9/11 attacks in New York. Herb has recently produced work for Eric Powell's *The Goon,* published by Dark Horse. www.herbtrimpe.com

HOWARD CHAYKIN has been amazing audiences not only as a comic book creator but as an illustrator and writer for television and film. His creations Iron Wolf and The Scorpion are major influences for Commander X. Howard led the way with the graphic novel format with *The Stars My Destination* and *Empire.* He's renowned for his groundbreaking series *American Flagg!* as well as revising The Shadow and Blackhawk for DC Comics. Recently, he created for DC's *Hawkgirl* and Marvel's *Blade*.

Special thanks to CHARLEY PARKER for his foreword. Besides being a great designer and artist, he practically invented webcomics with *Argon Zark!* www.argonzark.com

And last, but not least, many thanks to ROY THOMAS. Roy is a legendary author, editor and storyteller. Currently, Roy is writing his creation, *Anthem,* for Heroic Publishing. His love of the Golden Age and its creators is reflected in his fanzine, *Alter Ego.* www.twomorrows.com

THE STORY BEHIND THE STORY

A kid in a raincoat, in a rowboat, with a parrot.

You've got to be kidding.

That was my first reaction when I was asked to work with Capt'n Eli. Luckily, in spite of my reservations, I looked deeper and discovered a whole other universe and the opportunity to create an odyssey. But I'm getting ahead of myself. Let's start at the beginning.

Capt'n Eli is a namesake. It affectionately honors Eli Forsley of Gray, Maine. He was known as Dr. Eli and, in his time, he was that and more. He served in the U.S. Navy in the Pacific during World War II. After the war, he earned his master's degree in social work and a doctorate of education. He was a pioneer in providing the mentally ill and disabled veterans a home where they could be a part of the community.

Before I get even further, I should tell you that Capt'n Eli is also a brand. A brand of soda and, more specifically, a root beer. Eli Forsley's root beer. Yup, an old family recipe.

You probably think I'll say it's the best I ever tasted. You'd be right and I wouldn't be lying!

Fred Forsley, Eli's son, named his own son Eli. Around the time his son was born, he decided he wanted to bring the family root beer to the world -- or at least to his home state of Maine -- so, in honor of his Dad, Capt'n Eli's Root Beer was created by Fred and his partner Alan Pugsley. The soda label (featuring a kid in a raincoat, in a rowboat, with a parrot) was developed by the designer of this book, Chris Hadden, and illustrator Bruce Hutchinson. Scott Doyle joined the crew as brand manager and a recipe for success was created!

Since the beginning, Fred saw the potential of Capt'n Eli to be more than just a brand mascot. His father was well known as a great storyteller and for his spirit of fun. That sense of fun was expressed in his root beer and Fred felt this same sense of fun could be instilled in an adventure story. Combining the two E's -- entertainment and education -- he saw how Capt'n Eli could be a positive addition to the world of children's entertainment. He hoped the character could be developed into an animated show for kids.

This is where I come in.

Fred took a look at my work. I have a little experience with comic books and animation.

Check out *Scrap City Pack Rats* on eBay. Even after a decade, they are considerably cheaper than *Action Comics #1*. But seriously, folks, *The Rats*, as they were affectionately called, were the first team of disabled superheroes and the series was produced with Goodwill Industries of Maine.

I also used to work for Tom Snyder Productions, art directing and animating educational CD-ROMs. Check out *Fizz and Martina's Math Adventures* sometime. I also helped get Fizz and Martina on television by contributing animation to *Squigglevision*, which aired on *ABC's One Saturday Morning*.

A kid in a raincoat, in a rowboat, with a parrot.

It didn't really sound as silly as I first let on (no sillier than other stuff I'd worked on!). But I still had my doubts. Could we create something that stood on its own? I gave it some more thought. The Lone Ranger, The Green Hornet and Captain Midnight were all created to entertain and sell a product. Why not Capt'n Eli?

"Let's make a pilot," Fred said. Exaltation and fear mixed. Television production is a dicey and expensive game at best. Okay, I was a little chicken, but I suggested we start slow.

"A placemat," Fred said. We decided to start with an activity placemat with games and comics for families to enjoy while waiting for their meals to arrive at a restaurant.

At first, we thought a storybook fantasy approach might work, a la Dr. Seuss. I suggested we add Barney (I love dogs!) and name the parrot Jolly Roger. Capt'n Eli had a crew and we were off! *The Great Root Beer Battle* was created (check out captneli.com). It was fun. It was cute. I had a hard time thinking up another placemat.

Capt'n Eli as a detective and inventor intrigued me. While many adore the adventures of a boy on a broomstick, The Hardy Boys and Tom Swift were the adventurers of my childhood.

The Mystery of the Haunted Lighthouse was created as our first comic book. People liked it, kinda like Scooby-Doo, some said. It still wasn't clicking for me so it was back to the drawing board.

What did I want to do? What could I do? How could I best serve the purpose of promoting the product and create something that could stand on its own? I thought about all the great adventure stories of myth. I thought about seafaring stories, Captain Nemo, and old adventure comic strips. I thought about Eli Forsley. I thought about fathers and sons. I thought about heroes, real and imagined. I thought about every cartoon and comic I ever loved. I thought about the web. *The Undersea Adventures of Capt'n Eli* began to form and grew into this book.

In the next book I'll go deeper into how the story was created and some of its influences.

Thanks for reading and drop me a note anytime at jaypiscopo@captneli.com.

Until then, **STAND BY FOR ADVENTURE!**

Eli Forsley, 1943